parents and caregivers,

Stone Arch Readers are designed to provide enjoyable reading experiences, as well as opportunities to develop vocabulary, literacy skills, and comprehension. Here are a few ways to support your beginning reader:

- Talk with your child about the ideas addressed in the story.

- Discuss each illustration, mentioning the characters, where they are, and what they are doing.

- Read with expression, pointing to each word. You may want to read the whole story through and then revisit parts of the story to ensure that the meanings of words or phrases are understood.

- Talk about why the character did what he or she did and what your child would do in that situation.

- Help your child connect with characters and events in the story.

Remember, reading with your child should be fun, not forced. Each moment spent reading with your child is a priceless investment in his or her literacy life.

GAIL SAUNDERS-SMITH, PH.D.

STONE ARCH **READERS**

are published by Stone Arch Books
A Capstone Imprint
151 Good Counsel Drive, P.O. Box 669
Mankato, Minnesota 56002
www.capstonepub.com

Library of Congress Cataloging-in-Publication Data is available
on the Library of Congress website.

Library Binding: 978-1-4342-2528-3
Paperback: 978-1-4342-3057-7

Summary: After Buzz misses the school bus twice, he invents a
new way to travel to school.

Art Director: Bob Lentz
Graphic Designer: Hilary Wacholz
Production Specialist: Michelle Biedscheid

Reading Consultants:

Gail Saunders-Smith, Ph.D.
Melinda Melton Crow, M.Ed.
Laurie K. Holland, Media Specialist

Printed in the United States of America in Stevens Point, Wisconsin.

092010   005934WZS11

BUZZ BEAKER
AND THE
RACE TO SCHOOL

Written by CARI MEISTER

Illustrated by Bill McGUIRE

STONE ARCH BOOKS
a capstone imprint

Buzz Beaker loves to make cool new stuff. He keeps his ideas in a special notebook.

Larry is Buzz's best friend. He helps Buzz test inventions.

Buzz's dog, Raggs, is always excited for new inventions.

School Bus Speed

$v \approx 55\,mph$

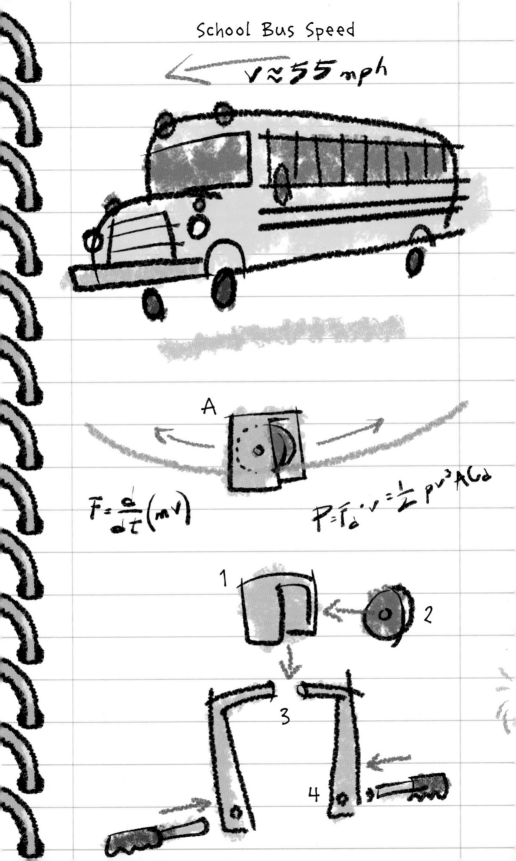

A

$$F = \frac{d}{dt}(mv)$$

$$P = F_d \cdot v = \frac{1}{2}\rho v^3 A C_d$$

1

2

3

4

It was dark. The Beaker
home was quiet. Everyone was
sleeping except Buzz.

Buzz loved the early hours of the morning. It was his best time to invent.

Buzz put on his goggles. He put on his gloves.

"Let's see how my formula is doing," Buzz whispered. His dog Raggs was still asleep.

Buzz poured green goo into a
jar. He added some liquid.

Then he stirred them together
with a glass rod.

Buzz frowned. "It's not quite right," he said.

Buzz mixed and mixed. He
was so busy, he didn't notice the
sun come up. He didn't hear his
alarm clock.

"Buzz! You're going to be late!" yelled Larry.

Buzz looked at his watch. "Oh, no!" he yelled.

Buzz grabbed his backpack.
He jumped out the window.

But he missed the bus.

Buzz ran all the way to school.
He was late.

Early the next morning, Buzz was working again.

"I have to figure this out," he said to the sleeping Raggs.

Buzz measured and poured.

Buzz mixed and stirred.

Buzz didn't see the sun. He didn't hear his alarm clock.

Buzz didn't notice the school
bus. "Buzz!" yelled Larry.
"You're going to be late!"

Buzz looked at his watch.
"Not again!" he said.

Buzz grabbed his backpack and jumped out the window.

Buzz ran fast, but he was late again.

Buzz walked into class.
Everybody was laughing.

"What is so funny?" asked
Buzz.

"I think you forgot
something!" said Sarah.

Buzz looked down. He could
not believe it! He was still
wearing his pajamas.

After school, Buzz put on some clothes.

"I can't be late for school again," he told Raggs. "I must think of something."

Buzz dug in his backpack.
He got out his notebook and
started planning.

"It will take two inventions.
But I know what to do,"
Buzz said.

Buzz found a hammer, a saw,
and a bell. Then he found a
very long piece of rope.

Buzz worked until dinner.

"There!" he said. "I'll never
be late for school again."

Early the next morning, Buzz was busy mixing. He was busy pouring and stirring.

He did not notice the sun. He did not hear his alarm clock.

But he did hear the bell ring!

"My invention worked!" said Buzz. "Now it is time to get to school!"

Buzz changed his clothes and jumped out the window.

Buzz missed the bus, but that did not bother him. Today he was not going to be late.

"Now it is time for my other invention," said Buzz. He grabbed a handle hanging from the tree.

He got a running start.

"Whee!" he yelled.

Buzz rode all the way
to school.

He was not late!

He even beat the bus.

THE END

STORY WORDS

goggles	liquid
formula	pajamas
poured	inventions

Total Word Count: 452

LOOK WHAT BUZZ IS BUILDING!